This book belongs to

Alicia Foster

Retold by Ronne Randall
Illustrated by Anna C. Leplar

This is a Parragon Publishing book
This edition published in 2006

Parragon Publishing
Queen Street House,
4 Queen Street
Bath BA1 1HE, UK

ISBN 1-40544-793-1

Printed in Indonesia

Hans Christian Andersen
The Emperor's New Clothes

p

Once upon a time there was an emperor who loved new clothes. He loved clothes made of silk and velvet and clothes made of satin and fur. He loved wool and taffeta and linen and lace. His tailors were busy making dozens of new garments every week.

Every morning, the emperor swept through the palace in brand-new clothes, enjoying the admiration of everyone he met.

"Your new ermine cloak is exquisite," his chief minister declared, bowing as the emperor passed.

"Indeed it is, Your Majesty," said the other ministers and courtiers, bowing in turn. They always said the same thing, no matter what they really thought. After all, no one wanted to upset the emperor!

One morning, the emperor told the chief minister to organize a grand parade to welcome some important foreign visitors.

"It will be a wonderful opportunity to show off a splendid new outfit!" said the emperor.

The emperor threw open his closet and gazed at the contents. After a moment, the emperor announced, "These clothes are all too ordinary! I want something EXTRAordinary. Something truly magnificent. Something no one has ever seen before! Find me the very best tailors and the very finest cloth in the kingdom!"

"Yes, Your Majesty," said the chief minister dutifully.

So the chief minister drew up a decree and messengers went to every corner of the land. The decree was read in every market square of every town. ——

"Hear ye! Hear ye!" the messenger proclaimed. "The emperor seeks the very finest, most talented, most gifted tailors in all the land. Anyone who can create a truly magnificent, extraordinary suit of clothes, unlike anything seen before, will receive a generous reward. Come to the palace next Thursday with samples of your cloth. Hear ye! Hear ye!"

Now, it just so happened that two rascals were in the crowd that had gathered in the marketplace to hear the decree. And they hatched a cunning plan.

On Thursday, a long line of tailors wound up to the palace doors. All of them had brought magnificent rolls of rich fabrics in brilliant colors.

But at the front of the line stood two tailors who seemed to have nothing at all.

"You shouldn't be here," said the chief minister. "The emperor only wishes to see tailors who have cloth to show him."

"We will leave if you insist," the two tailors said, "but we have been tailors to kings and princes all over the world. We have something very special to show the emperor, something no one has ever seen before."

Impressed, the chief minister ushered them into the palace.

The two tailors stood before the emperor, holding out their arms.

"This, Your Majesty," said the first man, "is the most amazing cloth in the world. It is so fine and delicate that it is almost invisible!"

"In fact," said his companion, "it IS invisible—but only to fools and simpletons. Anyone with wisdom and good sense can see how rare and beautiful it is."

Of course, the emperor could not see anything—because there was nothing there! The tailors were actually the two cunning cheats who had come to trick him.

Not wanting to look like a fool, the emperor said, "Yes, this cloth is magnificent. Don't you agree, chief minister?"

And the chief minister, who didn't want to look foolish either, said, "Yes, Your Majesty."

The emperor immediately ordered a new outfit made of the splendid cloth. All the other tailors were sent away, and a workshop was set up for the two cunning rascals. They asked for payment in advance, so the emperor gave them a purse filled with coins.

"First we have to weave more cloth," they told the emperor, "so we will need a loom and the finest gold thread in the kingdom."

When the loom and thread were brought, the two tailors got to work. Hiding the gold thread in their knapsacks, they began to "weave." But of course, the loom was empty!

The next day, the two tailors came to measure the emperor for his new outfit. One busied himself with the tape measure, while the other spoke to the chief minister.

"The emperor is such a fine figure of a man," said the first tailor, "that we will need even more cloth than we thought. We must have more money and more gold thread."

"Of course," said the chief minister, handing over another bulging purse.

"In this suit, you will look more handsome than ever before," the second tailor assured the emperor. "Your visitors will be amazed—unless, of course, they are fools and simpletons!"

"Of course," said the emperor, smiling nervously.

For the next few days and nights, the two rascals stayed in their workshop, keeping the doors locked.

As the day of the parade drew near, the emperor began to grow anxious.

"Go and see what the tailors are doing," he told his chief minister.

The two cunning rascals refused to let the chief minister in.

"It will spoil the surprise," they told him. "But if you give us more money, we can finish the suit sooner."

The chief minister handed over another purse filled with coins, then went back to the emperor.

"The new suit is beautiful," he told the emperor. "I am sure you will be pleased!"

The day of the parade arrived, and the tailors were summoned.

"Your new suit is ready!" they told the emperor proudly. "Here it is!"

As the emperor undressed, the tailors pretended to hand him his new clothes. And the emperor carefully pretended to put them on.

He pretended to step into the trousers…

…and he pretended to fasten them at the waist.

He pretended to put his arms in the sleeves of the tunic…

…and then he pretended to button all the buttons.

Finally, the two rascals pretended to tie the cloak around the emperor's shoulders, and to straighten the long train.

As the emperor strode proudly through the palace corridors, the palace courtiers and servants bowed and murmured words of praise.

The important foreign visitors were shocked to see the emperor wearing nothing but his wig and crown. And though they raised their eyebrows, nothing was said. No one would admit that they could not see the magnificent new suit of clothes. They all knew that the clothes were only invisible to fools and simpletons, and no one wanted to be thought a fool!

A huge crowd gathered to watch the grand parade. Everyone wanted to know if their friends and neighbors were simple fools who couldn't see the emperor's new clothes.

At last the royal procession came into view. The important foreign visitors walked in front, followed by the emperor's most important ministers.

Finally, a fanfare of trumpets announced that the emperor was coming.

A gasp rose from the crowd—but it was quickly followed by cheers.

"Look at the emperor's magnificent new clothes!" people cried. "Look at the fine cloth! Look at the colors!"

At the back of the crowd, one little boy hopped up and down to see the emperor's magnificent new clothes.

Finally, the little boy pushed his way to the front of the crowd.

"The emperor has no clothes on!" he cried, pointing and laughing. The crowd fell silent. Then someone called out, "The boy is right! It's true—the emperor has no clothes on!"

Soon everyone in the crowd was saying it: "The emperor has no clothes on! The emperor has no clothes on!"

The emperor knew that they were right. He blushed with embarrassment. "I didn't want anyone to think I was a fool," he thought, "but I have turned out to be the biggest fool of all."

And so the emperor just kept walking stiffly, staring straight ahead. He never even saw the two cunning rascals sneak away, laughing and clutching their bags of gold.

The End